MYSTERY OF THE FOXCREEK CREATURE

ROBERTA SAMS

DEDICATION

This little book is dedicated to my grandson Todd, and to my granddaughter Tara.

INTRODUCTION

We lived in a large metropolitan city during our working years, and when my husband retired we decided to move south to Florida, where we lived on the beach for a time. After a few years had passed my husband went to the local hurricane seminar presentation, and a TV meteorologist spokesman told the group that they lived in a serious situation.

"You folks are sitting ducks-- you live at sea level." He told them. "Because you live at sea level, it stands to reason that you are going to need to evacuate at some time and you may find it necessary to get off this island in a hurry."

There is only one interstate highway going north, and several winding narrow roads. But with the millions of cars that would be required to evacuate at the time of a disaster it was speculated that all those roadways could become parking lots and nobody could get anywhere. The discussion continued for a while, then it was suggested that some people could go inland a bit and wait out the storm. If one drove just thirty miles inland the elevation rises to 26 feet above sea level. Twenty six feet is not a lot of security when you think about the mountains of North Carolina and Tennessee, but it could help tremendously during a storm surge.

Anyway, that is how we ended up in Foxcreek. We had lived in the big City, then moved to the Beach but were unprepared to live in the interior of the state. It was the backwoods, without the mountains and trees. The land was flat and overgrown with bushes and scrub brush –there were marshlands and thickets. The road to Foxcreek was two lanes only for over thirty miles and the traffic was real slow. Upon arrival we found there were wild critters here that we weren't familiar with--unusual animals-- like armadillos and palmetto bugs. We saw buzzards the size of turkeys here, alligators and wild hogs could be seen as well; and there were lizards and snakes and strange sounds in the night.

There were pleasant things as well. An osprey would visibly nest nearby. Storks and pink feathered spoonbills frequented a pond in Foxcreek. And there was the daily morning visit of the ibis clan that gracefully landed and surveyed every lawn in the neighborhood surgically removing grubs and worms with their amazing beaks.

But the noises in the night were an unwelcome part of our transplant to this wildlife haven. We couldn't sleep because of this thing just outside our window that screamed out most of the night, then after several hours there would be silence until tomorrow when it got dark again and the yelling would pick back up.

That's how I came about writing the Foxcreek Creature. Foxcreek has been a most interesting adventure. Roberta Sams

1

THE CREATURE OF FOXCREEK

You don't see it, this creature of Foxcreek. In the daylight hours it hides itself in some obscure place among tall swamp grasses or in the trees and surrounding undergrowth. No one knows for sure where the thing keeps itself in the daytime but when the sky grows completely dark it emerges. Some say it comes alive at night, I don't know. The creature of Foxcreek is known by its loud shrill screech or maybe it's a howl, or a growl. We aren't sure how to describe its call. Some describe the sound as something like "mmmeeLP," with emphasis on the "LP." Others say it's a definite growl. Anyway, this creature begins its call across the wetlands about nine in the evening and it generally continues until the break of dawn.

Folks have considered whether it's a bird or not. Although they studied different bird calls and found that none matched the Foxcreek creature's nocturnal howl, yet these bird watchers actually think this thing is just another bird. The creature's call is generally piercing and penetrating, and it doesn't sound anything like any kind of bird you'd ever want to meet. Yet, they still argue that it's a bird--

allowing that it might be an unknown species. Of course he could have a bad-temper nature and that would cause his call to be different than the pleasant sound of a song bird or meadow lark. "Take the Whippoorwill for instance," they argue. "It doesn't sound like your normal bird call – and most of the time people hear the Whippoorwill but they don't ever see it, because it blends in with the landscape. Now your creature here is just another bird and although it doesn't chirp in a pleasant musical note like one would expect a bird to do – it's still a bird."

Ordinary people think that is a stupid idea and say that it's probably just a frog and it doesn't sing, it croaks. Frogs have no feathers and they don't have wings to fly either, and that's why once it has selected its site for the evening it stays there. If the thing is heard in a particular tree at nine in the evening, most likely it'll stay there until just before dawn. But tomorrow night it'll be somewhere else. It's the same night after night. Yes, this creature is much more than a mere frog. And searcher beware, you won't find it where you expect it to be.

Some people have gone out there with flashlights and felt the dampness of the night and experienced cold and hot sweats when a real genuine "hush" closed in around them. Many folks reported that the only sounds they heard were the sounds of themselves breathing. On one occasion some men reported that their feet "froze" to the ground and their legs failed to move although they tried to run. Understandably, once they got going they split. They threw down their flashlights and didn't even come inside the shelter but headed straight for their cars and left the swamp, never said "goodbye" or anything. They came back another day and told it all down at the general store.

If you go looking for the creature he shuts up and everything gets quiet ... spooky quiet all around the marsh. Of course, you can see nothing unusual and you hear only twigs cracking underneath your feet ... and your own quickened heartbeat. Shh... Just walk about two yards toward where you think he is and then stand very still for a few minutes and you'll find that the darkness becomes amazingly silent ... and that's about the time most people get out of there. It's not until after folks are safely inside the shelter that the squawking or shrieking picks up again and it's still coming from the same location as before. The thing hasn't moved ... it saw you ... but you didn't see it.

Dozens of outsiders have come to try and find the Foxcreek creature, but he has deluded them all. Most are scared to death and thankful to get out of there after a short time in the swamp. Several confessed that they tried to scream but they couldn't make a sound, however some of the neighbors over in the next county claim that they hear screams coming from the swamp pretty regularly.

One old man and a few kids think this is some kind of swamp creature that's mad about all the building and construction going on near its home. They liken it to a swamp type of bobcat or panther that could climb tall trees and wouldn't be scared off by flashlights or approaching footsteps. When it was pointed out to them that the sound this creature makes is "mmmeeLLP" and that that sound was not particularly peculiar to bobcats or panthers, they figured it didn't matter since it would have to be a mutant kind-of creature. That being the case, who knows what it sounds like anyway? Who knows what it looks like?

Granny Higgins, down at the post office, said that wasn't so. She said, "God made everything and everything He made was good. God don't make no mutant cross-breed anything. If this creature is mean and evil it got that way after it was born … or hatched … or whatever." She said she wasn't scared of the swamp thing no matter what it turned out to be. However, she did mention that she locked her doors after dark and prayed.

It was reported that the other night the Foxcreek creature had a buddy. The creature began shouting his loud and shrill "mmmeeLP" from an easterly location about nine o'clock, when about half an hour later there was a response from a position toward the west. Of course we didn't know how far apart they were, but we could tell that one was on the right and the other a good bit to the left from where we listened. We called the buddy Rubber Ducky, because he sounded just like my old rubber duck did when I squeezed him ... "squeak."

These two shouted back and forth across the marsh, "mmmeeLP, squeak, mmmeeLP, squeak, mmmeeLP, squeak " until the birds began chirping at dawn. After nine or ten hours of squawking and squeaking, the creature and Rubber Ducky stopped. It's that first spark of daylight that sends him running for cover. We thought the conversation between these two would pick up again on some future night but it didn't. Fact is, we never heard from Rubber Ducky again. We don't know if he just left to find his own territory, or if the Foxcreek creature ate him.

I suppose this riddle will be with us for a long time. But as long as the Foxcreek creature continues to roam the marshlands of southwest Florida, folks will be trying to track him down. Although we may never learn who or what the Foxcreek creature is, we know where he is ... we just can't find him.

2

A few of the townsfolk at Foxcreek got together and decided they would try to catch the creature. Grandpa Jake, Uncle Jim and even Mr. Hanson thought to make a trap for him. It would be a cage with a door that would drop-down once he was inside. At first they thought to make one with wooden bars, but after discussing that idea, it was settled on to go to the hardware store over in the county seat and buy a strong wire cage.

They would draw straws to see which one of them would be the person to drive over there and get the cage. Uncle Jim drew the short straw, so he would be the one to go. Matthew, who just entered fourth grade at the elementary school got wind of what was going on and he begged Uncle Jim to let him go with him to look for a trap. At first Uncle Jim said, "No." He didn't want any fourth grader telling him what he ought to do. Then after a while he gave in and decided to let Matthew go along, after all it might be good to have someone to talk to on the trip over there. Tomorrow was Saturday and there was no school, so they both got up early the next morning, and Uncle Jim put his ol' dog Blue in the truck and they set out for the hardware store.

The clerk at the hardware store told Uncle Jim that he had just the thing to catch the creature. It was a sturdy wire cage that you set out near where the critter is expected to be, and inside he told Uncle Jim to put a piece of fresh meat, like a piece of steak or something and prop the door open. The cage is designed that when the animal enters to get the meat that a trap-door springs shut and the critter is trapped inside. He brought the cage out for them to look at, but it seemed so small, it wasn't much bigger than a shoe box.

"What if the critter is bigger than the cage?" Matthew wondered. "If he's bigger than the cage you can't catch him in it."

"We don't know if he's bigger than the cage." Uncle Jim answered. "But maybe we'd better look at a larger size." He told the storekeeper.

The clerk went back to the stockroom and came back empty-handed. "The only other cage we have that can be used as a trap is pretty big. You probably won't want something that size." He said.

"Well, how big is it?" Uncle Jim asked.

The clerk took them to the backroom to see the cage. It was real big. It was so big that Matthew figured he might be able to fit into it if he tried.

"I don't know about this one either." Uncle Jim thought.

"But what if the creature is a lion or panther or something?" Matthew asked.

"Don't let your imagination run away with you, son, we don't think he's anything like that."

"But that's the only cage available, I suppose I could order one from the factory but it might take six weeks or more to get it."

It was a sturdy cage of strong steel wire and it could catch a small critter as well as a much bigger one. Uncle Jim decided to take the big cage, and asked the clerk to go over the set-up instructions again. And they loaded it into the pick-up and headed back to Foxcreek.

A cage sounded like an excellent idea, and seemed the perfect way to catch the critter. Yet no one thought about what they'd do with him if they did catch the Foxcreek creature in that trap. It didn't occur to them that the creature might be mean and vicious and mad because he had been caught.

He brought the trap home and Matthew and the three men went to Slim's grocery to get a piece of meat for the bait. They then went out into the swamp to set up the cage close by where they'd last heard his call. They gathered some dry grass and put it over the cage to kind of cover it up so the critter couldn't know it was a trap. He wouldn't see the cage but he would be able to smell the fresh meat inside and that's how they hoped to get him.

It was beginning to get late when they finished setting up the trap and Matthew went home, while the others stopped at the Cozy Kitchen and drank coffee and ate cake as they talked about what they had done. And they needed to discuss what they would do if and when they did catch the Foxcreek creature.

"Why don't we call the animal shelter over in the next county?" Mr. Hanson asked.

"We can't do that," Grandpa Jake declared. "You know what they do to dogs and cats, don't you? They put them to sleep, that's what they do."

"They wouldn't do that to the Foxcreek creature, would they?" Uncle Jim wondered.

"I don't know, but I think we should take him to the zoo." They were talking so fast now, that it was hard to tell who said what. "What would the zoo want with anything that makes all that noise and keeps all the other animals awake?"

The discussion went on for a few hours, and after a while the Cozy Kitchen closed up and they had to leave.

Early the next morning Grandpa Jake and Uncle Jim went to check on their trap. Mr. Hanson didn't want to go, he told them he was afraid to see what was in the cage. They walked slowly and carefully trying not to make any noise as they came upon the spot where the trap was hidden. Uncle Jim went on a little bit ahead and came to the cage first.

"We've got him, Jake." He called out.

Grandpa Jake speeded up a little bit and they knelt down by the cage and pulled back the grass covering.

"My word," exclaimed Grandpa Jake. "We caught us a raccoon."

"That's not the Foxcreek creature, it's just an ordinary raccoon. And he ate our bait, he ate that piece of steak we bought to catch the creature…. Now what are we going to do with a raccoon?" Uncle Jim wasn't a happy camper.

These trappers felt they had been outsmarted, but they thought they would try again tonight. They took the cage over to the creek and released the raccoon, who seemed happy to be free after spending the night in a safe cage and enjoying a nice piece of rare steak.

The following evening the two of them set up the cage on the opposite side of the tree to where it was the night before. They placed another piece of meat inside, left the trap door open, and covered it all with grass once more. They looked around and smiled, nodding their heads that they had it right and tonight they would get the big catch. They would trap the Foxcreek creature.

The word had gotten around town that these two men were close to catching the Foxcreek creature. Kids were becoming interested in the venture, and their parents were excited about it as well. They were asking so many questions, and most of them couldn't sleep for wondering if they'd really get to see the creature in the morning.

It was early when Grandpa Jake and Uncle Jim got up and put on their boots to go check on their trap. They had company this morning though; Matthew was there this time for it would be several hours before school started. A few other residents followed them out in the early morning dew toward the swamp, actually there were ten of them. Two ladies were in their housecoats with curlers in their hair. Some brought their coffee cups with them. Even Mayor Jones came and he brought a camera; he wanted to be the first to get a picture of the creature. He said he wanted to send it to the City Press so it would get in the paper and everybody could see the Foxcreek creature.

As they neared the place, there was a growl heard coming from the covered cage. Another growl was heard as they got a little closer. Grandpa Jake stood behind holding Matthew back a bit, and Uncle Jim went on ahead and began to take the grass off the trap. By this time all the people with them were gathered together waiting for the unveiling of the cage. They did stand back a little because they were concerned about his angry growl.

"Well, what in the world…." Uncle Jim gasped as he removed the grass. "How did you get in there?"

"What is it? Who is it?" Everyone wanted to know. And then Uncle Jim cleared the cage and everybody saw who was in there. And it sure wasn't the Foxcreek creature. It was ol' Blue, Uncle Jim's dog.

"This is the most ridiculous thing I've ever seen," a woman was heard saying. "I got out of bed at daybreak to come down here and get all wet in this dew thinking to see the Foxcreek creature, but all I see is a dog in a cage."

Mayor Jones was disappointed too. He didn't get a picture to send to City Press and Foxcreek wouldn't get in the newspaper.

But Grandpa Jake, Uncle Jim and Matthew were the most disappointed of all. They figured the Foxcreek creature had tricked them again. I guess they thought the critter conspired with the raccoon and the dog and got them to get into the cage and trick the trappers. They had been outsmarted twice, and they didn't dare go for a third time.

"Can we try one more time?" Matthew asked.

"No Siree." Was the answer he got.

3

Things have been jittery around Foxcreek lately for it seems the Foxcreek creature got everybody all stirred up. It all began when some kids happened to come across several pieces of chewed up rabbit fur and its other remains in a nearby field. If that was the only thing it wouldn't be enough to mention, but the way it turns out that isn't near all the evidence that is being stacked up against him.

Miss Collins had been at the PTA meeting all evening and it was around 9:30 when she got home. She went to bed, but was awakened later that night by an unusual noise outside and got up to look around. She swears that she saw the front-door knob turn and that's what scared her half to death. She called the sheriff who came with a deputy, and they searched all around her place and didn't even find a single clue. Well, guess who got blamed for that incident?

Sissy and her parents were visiting their relative the mayor, for a few days. They said they came from the north to visit uncle mayor, but the real reason seems to be the Foxcreek creature for they asked so very many questions of anybody who would talk to them. They questioned what he was like, how does he sound, and where does he live? They wondered if he really did those things that the people charged him with. They wanted to know everything about the creature. Billy Ray was showing Sissy around the marshland and helping her understand all the gossip and to kind of defend the critter.

They stopped to rest near a creek that ran along the edge of Foxcreek. "That's probably how the town got its name for there were foxes in the area at one time." He told her. "We haven't seen any, but foxes may still live here somewhere in the undergrowth."

There was a bench by the creek where one could sit and fish or just sit as these two thought to do. There were fish in the creek waters and sometimes you might spot a baby alligator if you were quiet and lingered there long enough. But it was beginning to get late, almost dusk, there was still some sunlight, although it would be dark soon. As they walked toward the broken pier they were startled to see a tall black figure maybe five feet tall, kind of slither off the bench and off the pier into the deep black water of the creek. They didn't hear a sound, no water splashing, nothing. They both blinked their eyes and looked at one another in disbelief before they ran all the way out of there.

"What on earth was that?" Sissy spoke as they neared the main street.

"I don't know, I don't know if it was the creature or not."

"Well, I think it was him." Sissy declared.

They reasoned between themselves that perhaps they had seen the Foxcreek creature.

Billy Ray remembered that someone in the next county had reported seeing an iguana that was six-foot tall standing upright. "Is that what we saw?" He wondered. "Reptiles never stop growing, so if one lived long enough it could grow to that tall --or that long."

Because of the surrounding circumstances, the whole neighborhood was beginning to question what or who this creature is? Is it dangerous? A lot of people were saying, "Yes."

Even Granny Higgins is beginning to have doubts about this swamp thing, especially since she found scraps from his fresh rabbit dinner in her back yard. We think she's the one who put up the wanted poster at the post office. They're offering to pay $100 dead or alive for the Foxcreek creature.

The sheriff came by the other day and voiced his concern that bounty hunters and crowds might jam-pack the area to search out the Foxcreek critter, and then he figured he'd get into real trouble with all the animal rights people. He'd probably lose his job if that happened, he said. "Now that there's a bounty on this critters head, I'm in a tight spot here; I have to protect this thing that everybody, including me, wants to get rid of."

Of course the election is not far away and our sheriff is no different than any other official that's seeking reelection. And that is, that you must try to please all the people all of the time until after the election, then you can resume your ordinary practices.

There are some in Foxcreek who think their sheriff reads too many mystery novels and especially too many western stories, how else would he be concerned about bounty hunters, and angry mobs trying to catch the Foxcreek critter so they could collect the $100. Somebody heard that he wants to deputize a few people just in case there is trouble so that he'd have his own posse waiting.

It all came to a head when a farmer discovered something had killed one of his calves, of course most everybody suspected the Foxcreek creature. Personally, I don't think it was. Then about two weeks after that Uncle Jim's dog got in a fight with something and got torn up pretty good. He wasn't too upset about the whole thing, said he figured that the dog needed it. Seems the dog was continually leaving home and looking for trouble, and Uncle Jim always said if you look for trouble you'll sure find it.

Word got around to the City Press fifty miles away. Somebody wrote an editorial in the newspaper suggesting that if the people of Foxcreek could catch the critter and send him to Miami or New York maybe he could blend in with all the people in the big city and nobody would notice him. That would seem to solve the problem for the village of Foxcreek and the critter wouldn't be hurt. It all sounded like a good idea, until somebody wrote a letter to the editor saying they thought that would be too cruel a punishment for the Foxcreek creature. And believe it or not, that letter echoed most people's sentiments, we actually like the thing, but wish it would be nicer.

All in all it is a bit tense around here. Mothers keep their children indoors all day and practically no one ventures outside after dark. Yet nightfall is the only time we can know his whereabouts. As long as we hear his "mmmeeLP" we know he's out there somewhere.

4

The mayor may have hit on something big at last month's town meeting. It seems that our town government is always broke, as all governments seem to be, but Mayor Jones is actually suggesting something that promises to put his town in the black and maybe even to profit way beyond that.

Actually the idea sprang from Miss Collins' fourth grade class. The kids wondered if they could just enjoy the Foxcreek creature and maybe celebrate his being in Foxcreek rather than discourage his presence. They wrote stories in the classroom and some even drew pictures of what they thought the critter looked like. It wasn't very long before every student wrote a letter to the mayor with his or her suggestion on how they could promote the Foxcreek creature in their neighborhood.

That's essentially how the idea moved from the classroom to city hall. It was now in the hands of the town council who discussed at length, what to do with all those letters from Miss Collins' fourth graders. At first they laughed, then some gasped, but things changed when one business man started seeing dollar bills and wondered why the city couldn't make the Foxcreek creature into a tourist attraction.

"We'll advertise in the City Press and all the newspapers up north and we can take out advertisements in the major travel magazines. People will come here in droves to see this critter—though ain't nobody seen him yet." He grinned.

When somebody questioned if that was fair, the group reasoned that they wouldn't promise that the tourists would see him, they'd just tell what they knew. "How many people do you know that have seen the Loch-Ness monster?" One of them asked.

Well of course none of them knew anyone who had seen the Loch-Ness, yet they'd all heard about it at one time or another. That issue was quickly settled and they began to discuss how they would go about making the Foxcreek creature into a celebrity, and more importantly, how would they handle all the visitors that would come to their quiet little village.

A team was appointed to spread the word about the Foxcreek creature. They figured it'd be easy to get it on the local radio station in the next town, after all it was news. Somebody would take pictures of the swamplands where they'd heard him, and others would write up advertisements for the newspapers and magazines.

Slim's grocery would make sure they had plenty of food for all the folks coming to town. And the Cozy Kitchen promised to open up a private dining room behind the kitchen so it could still serve home cooked meals to Foxcreek residents, while their main dining room would be converted into a hotdog and soda pop stand to serve all the expected tourists.

Miss Collins' fourth grade class and some third graders offered to make all kinds of Foxcreek creature trinkets to sell as souvenirs. Some of them volunteered to cut pieces of swamp grass and braid them together to make necklaces, bracelets and belts. They planned to cut and paste colorful pictures from magazines and collect sea shells to decorate their swamp grass creations. Grandpa Jake said he knew how to weave hats from palm- tree fronds, and he offered to make a few of them to sell.

The third grade art class had already drawn pictures of what they thought the creature might look like and they wanted to have an art fair and sell their paintings. Uncle Jim thought he could make picture frames for the student's art-work, and it would bring a better price. And some older students volunteered to park cars and direct traffic. Everything was seemingly coming together.

"It'll all work out perfectly, you'll see." The mayor gleamed.

5

The community of Foxcreek doesn't have a newspaper. Just a few people live there and if there's any news it gets around by word of mouth. Every now and then somebody puts up a notice at the Cozy Kitchen or down at Slim's store. Everybody knows that you can't put up a notice at the post office though – its government property. The town council members were correct in their assumption that people would come in droves to see their new celebrity. For after news about the Foxcreek creature was sent about, tourists and reporters came pouring into Foxcreek from a hundred miles away.

That news reached all the way to Orlando, and the newspaper there sent their top journalist to report on this new find. The kids thought he looked a lot like Crocodile Dundee because he wore a big straw hat and had a Dundee type knife strapped on his belt. He had real dark reflecting sunglasses so that when you looked at him you saw yourself. There were several pens in his shirt-pocket and he carried a big expensive camera around his neck, with extra film in his pants pockets. All in all he did look kind of funny standing there in his Hawaiian print shirt, kaki Bermuda shorts and hiking boots, with a clipboard in his hand.

He introduced himself as the reporter from Orlando and that he was there to get the full story on the Foxcreek creature, and he wasn't leaving until he got to the bottom of it. Apparently that didn't take long, for shortly after he arrived and looked around a bit he got into his brand new Jeep Cherokee and drove away-- but not before he dropped a hint that Hollywood might have an interest in the creature, and he wanted to be the first to get the scoop. If it was all that important we don't understand why he left in such a hurry.

Some of the women had fixed up their spare bedrooms and cooked eggs, smelly fish and swamp cabbage for their overnight guests, and called it a quaint bed and breakfast, "swamp style." Several news reporters and lots of tourists came and paid $100 a night for bed and breakfast in Foxcreek, and were happy to get accommodations. It was both a joke and a puzzle to the folks at Foxcreek though, they couldn't believe how many people came—and they didn't care how much it cost. This was a new adventure, a new "find," and they meant to be the first to get in on it.

The City Press came to interview Grandpa Jake. One of the first things the reporter asked was if Grandpa was afraid of the Foxcreek creature. Grandpa talked for two days on that one and the newsman was really sorry that he asked. But Grandpa wasn't afraid of the Foxcreek creature, nor anything else.

"No sir. I wouldn't be scared if Bigfoot walked by here," He said. "You city folks scare too easy…. I respect this thing but I'm not shaking in my boots afraid of it. Now you take young Hanson, who lives over there, that man is afraid to go out of his house… he's a nervous wreck— afraid of living and scared of dying…."

The Press newsman didn't have a chance to say anything as Grandpa continued talking about his neighbor, Mr. Hanson.

"I see a U-Haul coming down the street, looks like somebody is moving." The Press man interjected.

"Yep, that'll be the Brown's. They said they couldn't take all that noise. All night long "mmmlp" or "ymmlp" however you interpret it. Theirs is the house closest to the swamplands. You can sit inside their living room with the doors closed and hear the creature loud and clear even over the noise of their window air conditioner. Why, the critter's squall even drowns out their television sound. They lasted longer than any of us expected."

"Have other people moved?"

"About three weeks ago we had a mass exodus from Foxcreek. All in one day three moving vans and two pickup trucks moved people out of here. And one family moved all their belongings in their four-door car. They had their mattresses tied on the top and a couch hanging out of the trunk—it was the funniest sight. If they couldn't fit anything in that car they left without it--and they didn't come back to get what was left either."

"I guess it's quiet here now." The newsman spoke.

"It would be if it wasn't for these tourists. Thank God the rush is over and done with. The business people here made a lot of money, but we all got tired of it real quick. It's been better for the last week or so because the tourist traffic has dwindled down to five or six cars a day."

"How many came at first?"

"Well, we had over 500 cars one day. We raised the price to park from $5 to $10 and the entry fee to the swamp from $6 to $12, and they kept coming. If we'd had these empty houses we could have rented every bedroom and more. People were trying to set up tents all along here—dozens of them wanting to stay up all night, till the sheriff made them leave."

The newsman wondered, "This is quite a business enterprise then…. What will the people do with the money that the Foxcreek creature has brought in?"

Grandpa thought for a minute and answered, "Somebody suggested that we build some kind of monument or put up a welcome sign at the entrance to Foxcreek in the critter's honor. But the sad thing is that we don't know what he looks like, so we can't make a statue of him like they did for Smokey the Bear. Some of the younger guys suggested building a bowling alley so we'd have some place to go and not have to listen to him—you know there's a lot of noise where people bowl and it might be louder than the critter's squall."

6

Billy Ray and his cousin, Matthew, were fourth graders at the elementary school. They had the unique idea that instead of going out to search for the Foxcreek creature, they'd just let him come to them. Of course they hadn't discussed this thoroughly with their parents although each had brought it up from time to time, but tonight Matthew was staying over at Billy Ray's house and it seemed a good opportunity for them to fine tune their plans and prepare for action.

Right after school Friday afternoon, the two boys put on rubber boots, took an ax, some grass cutting shears, and a few other tools, and headed for the swamp. They were wise enough to walk through the backyard at the old Brown's place, that way they could get farther into the territory and avoid a lot of undergrowth doing it. Just a few yards beyond the Brown's fence the ground began to get real mushy and after a bit of hesitation they retreated a little and decided to set up camp where the grass and scrub brush was still dry. Matthew mentioned that they ought to camp close by a tall pine tree in case some wild boar came running toward them, then they could climb the tree and get out of its way.

Billy Ray laughed about that but they did pick a place close to a tree, it might come in handy to hang stuff on its limbs. They used the ax and shears to cut away some of the undergrowth around their proposed campsite for they knew that when they returned it would be dark and this swamp would be alive with all kinds of nightlife. They worked feverishly and without saying a word until a good-sized square parcel of ground had been cleared of all vegetation. When they finished they nodded approvingly, picked up their tools and left. They walked to Billy Ray's house in silence and washed up before supper.

After they ate and excused themselves, Billy Ray put on his rubber boots again and got his uncle's camouflaged shirt from the closet. Billy Ray knew how to do everything with style. He was just a few month's older than Matthew, but he seemed years older, at least to his younger cousin.

It was about eight-thirty when they reached their campsite. They brought folding chairs, four cans of Pepsi in a cooler, some bug spray, and of course a flashlight. It was just beginning to get dark, yet it wouldn't be totally dark-- although there were several black clouds in the sky, there would be a full moon tonight. Matthew was kind of glad there'd be some moon-light, he would be able to see a little bit anyway. But Billy Ray hoped it would be pitch dark.

"The creature may not show up since it'll be light out." He worried.

They set their chairs up on the cleared ground. The night sounds were beginning to start up all around them, there were frogs and crickets and other noises, but nothing that sounded like the Foxcreek creature was heard. They got out the bug spray as the mosquitoes came alive and began buzzing them. The boys quickly settled down on their chairs and opened a couple cans of pop and after a while Matthew dosed off as the lightening bugs flickered overhead.

The clouds moved in and covered the moon completely and as Billy Ray hoped it was totally dark now—no moon light, no stars nor anything. His ears perked up at the sound of a "swoosh" and a scratching sound, like bark being clawed off a tree. Then he heard a rustling, like the rustling of tree branches and it was coming from the pine tree just overhead.

Billy Ray tried to call to Matthew, but he couldn't speak. He opened his mouth but the words wouldn't come. He tried to yell for his dad, but it was no use. He had a nightmare once where he was scared half to death and tried to scream, but he couldn't make a sound. And he couldn't make a sound now, and this wasn't a dream it was for real. His hand was shaking so much that when he reached for the flashlight he knocked it over on the ground and it rolled away from him.

He tried to be very quiet and still crawl around on the ground to locate his flashlight, but it is so dark he can't see anything. He bumped his head into Matthew's chair, turning it over and spilling out a sleeping Matthew, who screamed at the top of his voice as he fell to the ground.

"Shh." Billy Ray found his voice and tried to quiet Matthew. "Something is in the tree overhead. Help me find the flashlight."

The two of them scrambled together there on the ground for the longest time before they found the flashlight. Billy Ray turned it upward toward the tree and they saw two big shining eyes staring back at them.

It's not too difficult to guess what happened next. Billy Ray and Matthew threw down that flashlight and ran away from there. They didn't bother taking their supplies; they practically flew all the way home, screaming every breath.

Outside lights were being turned on at each house they passed, and people began closing their window shades. When they got home there were half a dozen or so Foxcreek residents waiting in the front yard, armed for action. One person was holding a butterfly net, another had a fishing pole, one had a baseball bat and another carried a big stick. They had rakes and hoes and a fly-swatter. It's hard to know what they were going to do with all those things unless they expected to try and catch it with the fishing pole and butterfly net; if it was mean they could swat it with the fly-swatter or the baseball bat and stick. Then, after all was said and done they could use the rake to clean up the place.

Of course it wasn't funny to Billy Ray and Matthew, nor was it very funny to the concerned townspeople. They were all thankful that the boys were safe and that nothing followed them back. After a short while everybody went home and to bed, but most probably didn't sleep that night.

What hurt Billy Ray more than his dad's stern lecture was that he failed to find the Foxcreek creature. He knew it was a good plan and it should have worked, but they didn't even hear a peep from the creature while they were there. Although after it was all over, Matthew insisted that he heard the thing laugh when they ran away. He'll tell you that it was the Foxcreek creature, no doubt about it.

7

There was quite a commotion on the school grounds
Monday. It was such a ruckus that the principal had to be
called in before order could be restored. It seems that
Matthew let the word out on his "meeting up" with the
Foxcreek creature. Then, as the kids started to gather
around, Matthew kind of got carried away with all the
enthusiasm and exaggerated about the Foxcreek venture.

Some of his classmates cheered and squealed, others
argued and eventually the inevitable happened. One boy
hit another because he laughed at Matthew's story. Most
of the students believed it all and fifteen of them wanted to
go with him the next time. Yes, Matthew became a hero in
their eyes. But Billy Ray was embarrassed with all the
notoriety that his cousin was getting and he stayed clear of
him.

"Did you really see it?" Somebody asked.

"I sure did." Matthew boasted. "I saw two of the biggest
and shiniest eyes I've ever seen looking down at me. And
it was huge … and black as midnight. It looked like a big
swamp panther to me … sitting way up there on that tree
limb. I could almost feel his hot breath on the back of my

neck as we ran off. And… and you know what? He laughed at us as we ran away."

"How did you see him, if it was dark? Another student wanted to know.

"Well, it wasn't all that dark. And we had a flashlight anyway."

"Did you hear him? What did he say?"

"The only thing I heard was him climbing the tree and jumping out on that limb. Boy, did that limb rattle and shake. And you better believe I heard him breathing. And I heard him laugh at us too. It was weird." Matthew exclaimed.

"Weren't you afraid he'd chase you when you started running away?" A girl wanted to know.

"Heck no, I never had time to think. He'd of had to be fast to catch us anyway, the way we were running. Man, we flew out of there."

That's about the time the principal broke up the get-together and said he wanted to see Matthew after school.

Well, Matthew served his time after school and eventually admitted to the principal and Miss Collins that he didn't really see the Foxcreek creature. He admitted that he had been asleep until his cousin awakened him. He did hold to his story of seeing two shining eyes in the darkness, however. "Like raccoon's eyes when they look at truck headlights," he said.

Unfortunately, he didn't have any proof that those eyes belonged to the Foxcreek creature and that was the problem. After he had some time to think about the whole thing he felt a little silly and a whole lot embarrassed and promised to tell the truth to all the students tomorrow morning.

The next morning after Matthew explained to the kids, one of the girls remarked that she, for one, still believed it was the creature.

"You don't have any proof that it was him, and you don't have any proof that it wasn't him either." She said.

He felt relieved that no one was mad at him for making up the story, and most thanked him for telling the truth. "I didn't think it was all true anyway." One boy said, "I just thought it was a funny tale. My folks don't think there's anything to this Foxcreek creature, and that's what I think. If it's anything, it's just a bird or a frog of some kind."

"My dad said it's a wild and crazy man that lives out there in the swamp." Somebody else offered. "Well, if he lives in the swamp he must be wild and crazy." Another student added.

8

Some town residents quickly tired of the influx of people who hoped to be the first ever to catch a glimpse of the Foxcreek creature. Most didn't appreciate the scores of folk who trampled down their flowers and bushes as they carelessly walked across lawns and tossed aside drink cans, candy wrappers and all kinds of trash on their way to the swamp. A clean-up crew was needed to follow each tour and pick up the garbage they left behind.

It had been about a week since they'd heard anything from the Foxcreek critter and some entrepreneurs were concerned about losing this new money maker. They wondered if tourists would refuse to pay for the tours and accommodations if he didn't show up soon. Too, they were afraid they might get bad publicity if they couldn't produce even a sound.

The town council met to determine what they ought to do. A number of residents showed up at the meeting and voiced their opinions about tourists that wreaked havoc with their lawns. They'd just as soon call the whole thing off, they said. After all they weren't getting any richer from all this. It was the business people that were making money. They appreciated the fact that the town council hired people to clean up the mess in their yards, but it was more than that. They liked it better before the town of Foxcreek became so well-known and widely publicized.

As it turned out, the town council said it was sympathetic with the homeowners, nevertheless, it voted to continue its tourism project. They did agree to put up railings and build a boardwalk from the parking lot past five or six houses on the way to the swamp entrance. They had been using the church parking lot. It was not only the biggest parking lot in town, it was the only parking lot in town. Foxcreek had a Baptist church and a Pentecostal church and they were built side by side. It was designed that way so they could both use the same parking facilities.

After the homeowners left the meeting, somebody on the council board got the idea to tape some night sounds around the Foxcreek area on his portable cassette recorder and then play the tape on a loud speaker that they could set up in the swamp.

"Why on earth would you do that?" It was asked.

"In case the creature doesn't show up, it won't be a total loss." A council member responded.

"Well the creature sure won't come if you go blastin' noises all over the place." Slim, the grocer reminded them.

The town council argued about that for hours and when the opposition began to weaken they finally decided that it would be OK if they didn't turn on the tape until ten-thirty or later. For if the Foxcreek creature came, he'd be there before that time. And they agreed to only turn the speaker on then if tourists were present. "It's only entertainment." They agreed.

Early next morning a team set out to run wire into the swamp several yards where they would set up a speaker. Slim agreed to play the tapes from his back porch.

That evening two of the council members went to the swamp on a mission – to tape all the sounds of the night. The temperature was hot and muggy, and they hung around for thirty or forty minutes swatting mosquitoes and wiping perspiration from their eyes before deciding it would be just as well to go on back home and leave the recorder turned on. It seemed a smart thing to do, to set up their battery powered recorder, turn it on and leave. It would shut off automatically when the tape was full, and that's what they did. They planned to return tomorrow morning and retrieve all the noises in the swamp recorded on that cassette tape.

The following morning, the tape team was well rested and really kind of proud of themselves. They would have made a whole hour of swampland sounds while they were asleep in their own beds. They congratulated themselves, that it was a lot simpler than waiting out there for something to make a noise and then trying to get it on tape. Yes sir, they played it smart that time.

They continued to congratulate themselves as they walked across the cool swamplands, still wet with the heavy morning dew. As they came closer to their destination they hastened their step a bit, being anxious to see what they taped.

But the tape recorder wasn't there. They circled the area several times, thinking the wind might have blown it over. They even parted the grass in a few places, but they found no sign of the recorder. No tracks—nothing visible that would indicate something had taken it.

What would an animal want with a tape recorder? Then again, what person would come out here after night in the sweltering heat and bombarding mosquitoes just to get an old tape recorder? It didn't make sense.

One of the men remembered that some other items had been reported missing over the past few months—a kid's baseball glove, and a toy football were either lost or missing and they had not been found.

It seems that both team members had the same thought at the very same time. "Uncle Jim's dog!" They raced to his house, and sure enough on the back porch all chewed up, there was a kid's baseball glove, a toy football, and a chewed up tape recorder!

"Maybe he didn't destroy the tape. Maybe it will still play." They wondered. But when they took out the tape it was all mangled and twisted into knots and pieces.

Uncle Jim was apologetic, he was very sorry that his dog had done all that. But that didn't solve the problem, the tape was completely destroyed. The team members said they were done with the project, and that they had no thought to try and get another tape.

9

The main street through Foxcreek was lined with anxious bystanders hoping to get a glimpse of the important visitor to their little town. They didn't seem to mind the slow drizzle on this grayish rainy day; they just wanted to see what a dignitary looked like. You might be surprised to know that the man in this long white limousine was hand-picked by the president himself. Mr. Knowital came all the way from Washington, D.C. to study the Foxcreek creature.

Because of the aggressive promotional tactics of some residents that hoped to get dozens of tourists headed in their direction, news about the "creature" traveled all the way to the nation's capital. Since it is election year and the white house is anxious for any new story to make its candidates look good, they thought the Foxcreek creature might help. The way we heard it was that they figured it couldn't hurt him.

Mr. Knowital is a research professor from Harvard or somewhere, we're not real sure where, but he is said to be quite knowledgeable in the study of wildlife and animal behavior. Because of the professor's expertise, the white house wanted him to take a look at our creature. They want him to figure out what it is and where it came from and in doing that he would score points for their political candidate. At least it would show that the nation's capital had an interest in small town America, and it would be a warm human interest story.

Everybody waved as his limousine passed by. The townsfolk stood on soggy grass and smiled as women's hairdo's drooped and mascara ran down their rain-streaked faces. Children laughed and yelled and some put their little wet and muddy hands on the car's windows in an effort to touch this important man. After a few yards, the windows became so smeared and dirty you couldn't even see who was inside the car. They all had hoped to shake his hand and hear him speak in his "foreign" accent but they wouldn't be able to, for he would only meet with the mayor and the town council.

Over the next two days, Mr. Knowital heard testimony of several of the townspeople that were considered most knowledgeable of the Foxcreek creature. That would probably be Matthew and Billy Ray and they'd probably tell him an elevated story—that's just a little bit bigger than they told anybody else. Of Course, Granny Higgins was the first one to testify and everybody figured she gave him a real good version of what she knew. He didn't question Grandpa Jake very much; it seems he wasn't in there more than fifteen minutes total.

After he had talked to the witnesses and asked whatever questions he wanted to, they said the professor packed his briefcase quietly and quickly, and he and his chauffeur got in the limo and left. He didn't tell anybody anything.

"We thought he was going to tell us what our creature is." Somebody heard Uncle Jim say.

"That's just not nice," Granny Higgins retorted. "I missed a day's work for this. You all know I just can't take off two or three hours whenever I have a notion to."

I guess Mayor Jones saw trouble brewing and he stepped in to try to head it off. "Oh, the professor will have to study his findings. I'm sure he'll let us know what he thinks when he sorts everything out." With that, everybody went home and waited.

The mayor was correct, for in a few weeks he actually received a letter from Washington thanking him for his participation in this study and low and behold it did include what they called their "preliminary findings." The mayor called a town meeting to read the report.

The people of Foxcreek crowded into the town hall and the mayor opened the envelope. The report was quite boring and it was long, seems like it was forty or fifty pages. We didn't read it all – we went straight to the "Conclusion" written in "layman's terms."

"After extensive research I have concluded that the Foxcreek creature is a reverse evolutionary species previously unknown to man. This is of peculiar significance since the normal evolutionary process begins with an amoeba and over millions of years therein it evolves to something like a tadpole then after several million more years to a frog or a fish then a few million more years causes it to grow wings and fly. After that it grows a tail and swings from trees in the jungle, and some millions of years later it becomes a man. But this Foxcreek creature has stumped the whole evolutionary system of study for my colleagues and I believe it to have started at a higher form and that it is reverting to something lesser...."

Well, somewhere about halfway through that reading the whole room broke up into laughter. Some laughed so hard their stomachs hurt.

"Looks like Mr. Knowital thinks he came from a monkey and the creature didn't." Grandpa Jake figured, while Granny Higgins clapped her hands and danced around and Slim was almost rolling on the floor.

10

It has been almost a whole year since all the hoopla and fuss over the Foxcreek creature began. The residents at Foxcreek have quieted down and their lives have somewhat returned to normal, whatever that is. Anyway, it is indeed more peaceful here and folks aren't constantly wondering when the next group of tourists will converge upon them.

The creature is still around however, and he can be heard now and then, but most of the people just seem to ignore him. They don't care as much now, or maybe it doesn't bother them anymore. I guess its old stuff, the past is past – been there and done that, and now they were ready to move on.

Oh, they still like him, some of the residents think kindly of the creature and when the nights became chilly last winter somebody took a quilt over to the swamp and spread it down where they figured he would find it. They said he did use it, for when they later saw the quilt it was kind of crumbled up like he had wrapped himself in it.

One can even follow a trail of empty McDonald's hamburger containers, and Wendy's carry-out bags all the way to where the creature is supposed to be. The clean-up crew is still needed to clean the mess in the area, just like they did when the tourists came. Of course nobody will admit that they would bring any snack lunch to the Foxcreek creature. They all condemn feeding the critter, saying it would just encourage him to stay around.

"It's like feeding a stray cat, once you feed him he won't leave, he is yours forever."

One evening, just before dark, Granny Higgins was seen carrying a hot TV dinner back to the swamp. Of course, she didn't say she was taking it to the creature when somebody asked her about it.

"I don't even like that thing," she replied. "Why would I want to take food to it?"

There's a good side to this story though, because with all the hand-outs the creature hasn't needed to hunt rabbit or squirrel or anything else, he just sits and waits for home delivery. Black bears and stray dogs may raid garbage cans, but the Foxcreek creature gets room service.

School is just about over for the year, and next year the fourth graders will be promoted to fifth grade. Matthew and Billy Ray and the others will have to board the school bus for the ride to school at Morning View about ten miles away. They have mixed emotions about leaving Foxcreek Elementary though, and going to the new school.

Of course their first concern is that they are leaving fourth grade and being promoted to fifth. But this is different, they even have to learn about another school building, and it's so big. They'll have to find out where the doors are, and the cafeteria and everything. They won't know any of the teachers, or the principal, everything will be new to them. It is a bit frightening, because they don't know what anything will be like at the new school.

"The school is so big, and I heard the principal is real mean." Matthew worried.

"But you will be able to have more friends." His Dad said. "Here at Foxcreek there are only fifteen students in Miss Collins fourth grade. There will probably be twenty-five or more in your class over there."

"That's what scares me." Matthew thought. "All those kids in my class and I won't know a single one."

We can understand that their attention is on many things these days, and the Foxcreek creature is not the one they're concerned with at this time.

He is most likely happy about that too. Because now he can continue being whatever he is, and doing whatever critters like him do. And now he won't have so much harassment with everybody wanting to find him, to see him, or just to hear him growl or snarl or call "mmmeLP."

The creature just wanted to be left alone, and maybe that is what will happen.

Made in the USA
Charleston, SC
23 March 2016